NUMAGICIAN

The Magic Numbers And Untold Stories

Written By FuSuSu - Nguyen Chu Nam Phuong

Can You Guess Which Animal I Am?

That is an old question you can find in any book related to Numagician, an ancient kingdom. I love asking that question because not many people can give me the right answer. If you think I am a bird or a parrot, it's partly true. Can you see the number 69 on my face?

I'm a number. People often call me Bird 69. Whenever you take a photo of me, you will always see me like that. Not only me, but every number in Numagician has this unique pose. Unfortunately, I can't take you there right away to meet those beautiful friends. However, I brought photos of them. Please take a look and guess what their names are?

Well, what do you think? Can you see the numbers hidden in their photos? The answer is somewhere in this book. Just keep reading, then the secrets will be revealed.

Besides the numbers that they represent, they are also inspiring teachers and helping Numagician people to be happy all the time. Classes in Numagician are full of laughter; students understand and memorize the lessons deeply. Our teaching principle is that when people open their mouths and laugh, the knowledge will go in their stomach and stay there a long time.

Oh, I wish you were there, to laugh happily and learn something useful every day. That wish has also bothered me for a long time because I honestly wanted to return to my hometown. Although I cried many tears, no god showed up to make my dream come true.

Later, a quote from my best friend helped me to regain my strength. "A dream is just a dream if you don't take action every day."

That quote inspired me to follow my dream every day, so I came up with this diary that is in your hand right now. I hope it will help you smile happily like Numagician people.

Besides, the small amount of money from selling this diary as a book will cover the cost of finding a way home to my beloved Numagician kingdom.

Before I begin, please understand that my hobby is flying around, so I will write about my Numagician friends in no particular order. Moreover, I will only talk about my best friends. You can find the others' photos at the end of this book to draw. You can even compose a story about each of them and compare it with mine when this diary's sequel comes out.

Are you worried about your writing skill? Don't worry; at the end of this book, a simple secret to creating compelling stories will be revealed. If you are ready, turn to the next page and meet one of my most inspirational friends.

Note: In Numagician, each number is a living animal, and there are a few ways to call their names. For example, my friend on the next page is a mouse which represents the number 92. On his ID, you can see his full name is "Mouse Ninety Two", but I prefer Mouse 92 for short.

Mouse 92
Keep Dreaming, Keep Going.

Mouse 92 is an author of many bestsellers, including "9 Tips to Make Friends with Cats", "2 Ways to Exercise with Mouse Traps," and "Capture Any Rice Jar in 92 Seconds." His greatest dream is not to become a bestselling author but a traveler singing around the world.

Mouse 92 is not good at singing, but he loves it. Even though everyone gave him a lot of advice, Mouse 92 kept singing passionately and tirelessly. He would sing everywhere, including the bathroom, the bus station, a bamboo bush, even on the beach. There is no place people were not *tortured* by his male-duck quacking voice.

I'm sorry if I hurt some ducks' feelings. It's the truth, and I have no other way of describing his voice.

Once, Mouse 92 sang in a park, and a strange thing happened. His voice made a baby grin continuously, and the mother couldn't breastfeed it.

The mother was distraught. She ran to Mouse 92 and said, "Hey, singing too much will get you a swollen throat, aren't you afraid?"

"Hey lady," Mouse 92 replied as if he was singing. "No one knows the future; why so pessimistic? From now until the moment my throat is swollen, every minute of worrying takes me 60 seconds to sing."

The mother realized that instead of wasting 60 seconds to get angry with Mouse 92, she could look at her child with joy. I always wondered why his singing voice appealed to the children? It could only be his whiskers. They were shaking while he was singing.

Another time, a policeman came to Mouse 92 with big handcuffs. "Hey, many people are complaining about you. Do you want to go to prison?"

Mouse 92 stroked his whiskers. "Hey, Officer, I can sing everywhere, even in prison."

Hearing that, the police officer left immediately without replying. Perhaps he foresaw the prison breaking rate would double if they equipped the prison with a new form of torture: Listening to Mouse 92's singing voice.

Later, the police officer found out that I was a close friend of Mouse 92, he asked me to give Mouse 92 some advice.

"Hey, Mouse 92. I know you love singing, but your voice is so bad."

Mouse 92 hummed, "Hey Sixty-Nine, please tell me. What is good? What is bad?"

I didn't know how to reply. Honestly, I rarely listen to music, so I don't know what a good song is or isn't.

"Uh, people said that... I just repeated to you what they said."

Mouse 92 laughed out loud. "Ignore me. If someone doesn't want to hear, why don't they cover their ears?"

I had nothing to say. I gave up. I flew to my home near the chicken farm, then enjoyed the rest of the beautiful Sunday.

While flying, I noticed a poor man hiding behind a nearby bush overhearing our conversation. He smiled happily, his eyes sparkling as if he had just found the truth.

Shortly after that, I heard he had become a billionaire with a chain of shops specializing in earplugs. His secret was following Mouse 92 to his favorite singing spot, then opening a shop there. Later, to make his company worldwide, he donated money to help Mouse 92 travel worldwide, sing and sell earplugs for him. He even bought insurance for Mouse 92's throat with millions of Susu (Susu is the money that is used in Numagician.)

Therefore, Mouse 92 fulfilled his dream. We have met less often since that time, but Mouse 92 still sends me gifts. His most significant gift was a box of 92 CDs, recordings of his songs about the mice's greatness. Of course, I never dare to play them because I'm afraid of the police officer.

At the end of that year, the forest managers organized a singing contest. They forced everyone to send in a CD recording of the best voice in their family. The organizers would play one disc per day for people to vote on. Therefore, I must record my duckling voice, then send it to them.

The next morning, I suddenly heard Mouse 92's voice on the loudspeaker. Come on, how did I send the wrong CD to them?

The management came to my house, banging on the door. I could only squirm in a dark corner, not dare to open the door. It wasn't until the policeman came and announced that I won the first prize in the contest, I opened the door to see what had happened.

It turned out to be real. The management even prepared a long-term contract, forcing me to record more CDs. Of course, I honestly declared that it was Mouse 92's voice and gave them the box of 92 CDs as well. Since then, our bird forest has been filled with the sounds of mice squeaking.

Later, I found out that Mouse 92 met many good singers who helped him improve his voice in the journey around the world. Currently, Mouse 92 still travels and sings but doesn't sell earplugs anymore. He is selling books, and the poor man is his manager.

The lesson I learned from Mouse 92 is to be optimistic in any circumstance and keep taking action on the path to fulfilling your dream. That's my lesson, what's yours?

Please take a moment to answer the question: How do you feel about Mouse 92? Please write down your lesson before we read about my next friend. I'd love to hear from you.

Lion 51
Unite Or Die?

Lion 51, is the best leader I've ever known. People continuously vote for him as one of the 51 greatest kings of the jungle. Thanks to him, everybody in my forest lives in harmony, including humans, animals, and numbers. Every time my grandchildren fight with each other, I tell them the story that Lion 51 told me.

In the past, when the name of the Numagician kingdom hadn't been decided, humans were not so friendly. They even hunted and ate other species. At that time, lions were the most powerful species, so they were assigned to protect the forests, with the title *King of the Jungle*.

There was an old lion king who had two sons in the jungle, and he had not decided his successor yet. The older lion was strong, with the ability to roar loudly, but he was too arrogant. The younger lion was lighting fast, but he was too meek, and his roar sounded like a rat squeaking.

When the king was about to die, he sent an eagle to summon his sons. He decided to choose his successor by a hand game named *Rock-Paper-Scissors*.

After flying a while, the eagle found the older lion. It swooped down and said, "Sir, the king is dying. He gave you and your brother the order to come back and join in a game named *Rock-Paper-Scissors*, the winner will be crowned. Where is your brother?"

"Thank you," the older lion said. "You can go home and rest. My brother is on the mountain, and only I know where he is exactly. I'll talk to him, and then we'll go to the palace."

After the eagle had gone, the older lion took a bucket and went up to the mountain. Later, the older lion found the younger brother practicing his voice near a stream, next to the bridge leading to the sacred mountain.

"Hey," the older lion said. "The king is about to die."

"Oh no!" the younger lion said. "We need to go right now!"

"Take it easy, bro," the older lion said, and handed him the bucket. "There is a holy lake on the sacred mountain. Please get the holy water to help our father clear dandruff on his mane. He wants to look clean to meet God."

Taking the bucket, the younger lion went up to the mountain. Later, the older lion broke the bridge and then returned to the king.

"Where is your younger brother?" the king said.

The older lion said, "He is washing his hands at the holy lake to get luckier in the rock-paper-scissors game."

The king was so angry, he had a heart attack and died. The younger lion didn't show up at the king's funeral, so the older lion automatically became the new lion king.

One morning while walking near the old stream, the older lion saw a few monkeys eating bananas next to the broken bridge. The older lion was afraid they could find the younger brother, so he roared to bully them.

"Hey monkeys, do you know who I am?"

The monkeys were startled. The monkey leader crouched and stepped toward the older lion. He bowed a few times then said, "You are the king of the jungle. No one can escape from your claws, not even humans!"

The older lion smiled in satisfaction and roared loudly. The monkeys ran in disarray, leaving bananas scattering everywhere by the stream's bank.

A few moments later, the older lion met the familiar eagle, hovering over the sacred mountain.

"Hey eagle!" shouted the older lion. "What are you doing?"

The eagle swooped down. "Sir, I heard a small roar. I think your brother is still alive. I'm looking for him."

The older lion said. "Have you forgotten who I am? Say that again!"

The eagle said respectfully. "Sir, you are the king of the jungle. No one can escape from your strong teeth, not even humans."

The older lion nodded his head. "Good. While crossing this bridge that day, unfortunately, the bridge was broken, so my younger brother must have died. There is nothing to do here. You must go back now."

Then the older lion roared. The eagle flew away in panic, leaving a few feathers floating in the air.

Another day, the older lion saw a herd of elephants near the stream. They were building a new bridge to get to the sacred mountain.

The older lion roared, "Hey, elephants! Do you know who I am?"

The elephant leader replied politely, "Yes, sir, you are the king of the jungle. No one can escape from your lightning jumping, not even humans."

The older lion was satisfied, and he roared one more time. The elephants cowered. Some elephants swallowed a log by mistake. They fell to the ground, shaking, then went to the hospital.

Therefore, the whole forest was afraid of the older lion. No one dared to approach the sacred mountain.

One afternoon, while touching his majestic mane in the palace, the older lion saw a monkey running frantically to meet him.

"Dear Lion King," the monkey said. "There are humans!"

The older lion frowned. "You are good at picking bananas. Why not make humans slip on banana peels?"

"Sir," replied the trembling monkey. "I'm too afraid. Only you can get rid of them."

Right after that, the monkey climbed onto a tree branch and disappeared. The older lion went out to see what had happened. He met the eagle packing as if preparing to go far away.

The older lion frowned. "Hey eagle, you have speed and a sharp beak. Why not give humans a fight?"

The eagle shivered. "Dear sir, I'm too scared. They have guns that shoot out terrible candies. Only you can fight against them."

Suddenly, there was a loud bang. Without saying goodbye, the eagle picked up his backpack and flew away.

The older lion went to the stream bank and saw a herd of elephants running. The fattest one was hobbling slowly. It might have slipped on a banana peel left by the monkeys in the past.

The older lion blocked the fat elephant. "Hey elephant, you are so big. Why not crush humans?"

"Dear sir, I'm frightened. They have dangerous grenades. Only you can beat them."

Then the elephant kept hobbling, and sometimes it slipped on a few more banana peels.

Only the older lion left, he bravely headed towards the river, where noises were thundering through the forest. When he saw a scrawny hunter, he roared.

"Hey! Do you know that I am the king of the jungle?"

The hunter laughed. "If you are the king, then where are your troops?"

The older lion did not have time to answer; dozens of hunters appeared with large guns from out of nowhere. Then a series of gunfire sounds rang out.

A day later, no one could hear the roar of the older lion as usual. The hunters kept trespassing through the forest. They built their barracks on the sacred mountain, hunted and ate every creature in the woods.

One beautiful day, while the chief hunter was cleaning his gun at the barracks' gate, he saw an elephant passing by. Noticing the elephant was not only big but also hobbling, he ordered the hunters to chase it. When they returned to the barracks, all guns and ammunition were taken away by the monkeys.

Then, a small lion roared in the bushes. They pulled out their guns and shot blindly. This lion was too fast. When they ran out of ammunition, they pulled out the grenades, but a flock of eagles swooped down, making them fall on the ground. The small lion roared again, every animal in the forest attacked at once.

The animal revolution was a big success. The forest became peaceful as usual. The little lion that day was the younger lion. When the hunters repaired the bridge, he returned and gathered his army, and trained them day and night, waiting for the opportunity to fight back.

Listening to that part of the story, I admire the younger lion's leadership skill so much. I wish the king were wiser, crowning him sooner. Perhaps the forest would be peaceful from the beginning, and many creatures would not have to die unjustly.

"Hey, Lion 51," I asked. "How was the younger lion after that?"

"He is my grandfather," Lion 51 replied. "He is also the man who came up with the name Lion 51 for me and trained me as a leader. He said each of the five toes on a foot is different, but they are on the same foot. Each species is different, but we live in the same forest. The duty of a leader is uniting them and making a strong foot."

"Great. Do you have a secret?"

"Oh yes. Roar less and do more."

The conversation with Lion 51 made me realize that I should also sing less and do more. I should spend more time on taking action and making my dream come true.

28

Rabbit 28
How To Create Time?

You probably know many famous inventors, but you certainly don't know Rabbit 28, the most wondrous inventor in Numagician.

Since Rabbit 28 was a kid, her passion has helped her invent many useful things, including a carrot as big as a warehouse and a blender that turns fruit into candies. Her most recent project is to build a spaceship and fly to the moon and give Ms. Moon carrots to decorate the moon.

I first met Rabbit 28 at an exhibition of inventions. At that time, I was engrossed in a strange alarm clock, with a bird that popped up and said, "Wake up, it's the end of the world!" or "Wake up! Sleeping too much will make you fat!"

Because I was so interested in those funny inventions, I had no idea that Rabbit 28 was standing behind me.

"Hey boy," asked Rabbit 28. "In your opinion, how do you create time?"

"Uh yes," I'm confused. "If even a wise person like you doesn't know, then only God knows. Why do you want to create time?"

"You see," Rabbit 28 sighed. "Our kingdom has huge carrots thanks to my knowledge of biology. We have blenders turning fruit into candies, thanks to my knowledge of physics. I was able to create many things because I understand the science behind them. But I couldn't understand how to create time."

"So, what are you going to do?"

"Perhaps I will pay God a visit."

Several days later, Rabbit 28 brought home a giant carrot and made a ship from it. The day she left, everybody was regretful because they could never see the exhibition of her interesting inventions again.

Several years passed, and Rabbit 28 had not returned yet. The science classes were closed, and no one was interested in creating new machines. Numagician Kingdom gradually became bleak without new inventions.

About Rabbit 28, she traveled everywhere, meeting all knowledgeable people in the world to ask that question about creating time. But the answer she always received was, "If even a wise person like you doesn't know, then only God knows."

A few more years passed. People said that she even reached Almagician, the kingdom of magic letters across the ocean, but there was no answer yet. Perhaps only God could help her.

Once resting under a tree, remembering youthful achievements, she fainted.

Waking up, Rabbit 28 looked around, and realized that she was floating, surrounded by clouds that looked like cotton candy. From a distance, she saw a large gate with dazzling light. The signboard read, "Thank goodness. Heaven is here!"

"Heaven?" Rabbit 28 panicked. "Am I dead? Is my time up? No way, I have to wake up!"

She wanted to turn back, but she kept floating like a balloon. Then a wind blew her toward the gate, smashing her whole body against a giant red bell.

A ding-dong rang out, the gate opened. An older man in a white shirt, flying on a cloud, appeared.

"Hello," he said.

Rabbit 28 looked at him from head to toe. There was a picture of the sun on his shirt. "You are…"

He smiled. "An old man with a sun image on his shirt. Can you guess who I am?"

"Are you God?"

"Exactly! People look at the sky and call my name all the time!"

Rabbit 28 laughed. She was surprised that she finally met God. Remembering her goal, she asked, "God, why can't I create time?"

God grinned. The sunlight from his bright teeth spread all over the place. He said, "If you can create time, will I be unemployed?"

Rabbit 28 said nothing.

"Time is the most precious gift I give to you every time you wake up. You used to spend your time well to serve all species. Why don't you continue to do that? Why waste a quarter of your life learning my magic?"

God laughed. His smile not only dispelled the dark clouds surrounding them but also the haze in the mind of Rabbit 28. She was enlightened. Her tears trickled down her white, fur cheeks.

"Don't worry," said God. "When I retire, there will be a contest. If you win, you can freely create time like me."

Rabbit 28 cried. Tears welled up in her eyes.

"Hey, don't cry," God appeased her. "If you cry up here, there will be rain down there. Did you know that?"

Rabbit 28 cried louder.

"All right," God sighed. "I'll give you a little more time. If you're going to cry like this, there will be a flood down there."

Suddenly, everything became dark. Rabbit 28 opened her eyes and found herself lying under a tree, looking toward the blue sky. She said, "Thank goodness, I'm still alive!"

Later, she set sail to Numagician. The day she returned, everyone greeted her with joy. Even some spiders in her lab welcomed her warmly by cleaning the web. After that, she spent the rest of her life creating more wonderful inventions for all species and teaching people how to use time wisely.

To adults or people who are always serious at work, she says to them: "You may not have enough time to do everything, but you always have enough time to do the most important things."

It means when you do the important tasks first, it's like putting a rock into a glass of water, then there is still room for pebbles and even sand. If you do the opposite, putting sand and pebbles first, there will be no room for the rock.

To children or people who are eager to have fun but refuse to work, she always reminds them: "Suffer first, enjoy later. Enjoy first, suffer later."

It means if you work first and then play, it might be painful at first, but later you can enjoy everything. When doing the opposite, you may be happy at that time, but you also might lose track of time, then the consequence will be miserable.

Thanks to the simple lesson of Rabbit 28, I have gradually had time for my hobbies such as sunbathing, hair dyeing, etc.

One most important thing she helped me realize was: Everyone has 24 hours a day. Instead of dreaming for an extra hour, spend your time wisely.

That's my lesson. What's about yours? Please write down your comments, and don't forget to apply this lesson to your life!

Eagle 57
Anyone Can Fly!

Some birds are small, and some are big. Eagle 57 is the biggest bird I've ever seen. I went through most K.F.C. restaurants here, and I couldn't find any chicken thighs bigger than his thighs. The most special thing is that Eagle 57 knows a foreign language. He can speak Chickenish (the language of chicken.) Why? Let me tell you.

Before moving to the mountains to live, eagles nested on the trees next to chicken farms in the old days. The main reason was to hunt; this way caused so many unfortunate incidents.

A tree was tilted on a stormy day, causing an eagle egg to fall into a chicken coop. That egg was Eagle 57. My home was nearby, so I witnessed this extraordinary story.

When Eagle 57 cracked out of his egg, everyone in the chicken family gathered and gave him the best compliments ever.

"Everyone!" the chicken dad exclaimed proudly. "Can you see how big his thighs are? What a potential chicken!"

"Everyone!" the chicken mom exclaimed. "Can you see how strong his wings are? What a potential chicken!"

"Every...one!" the chicken grandpa whispered. "Can you see how big his butt is? What a potential chicken!"

Eagle 57 was so happy. He had a strong belief: "I'm a potential chicken!"

Just like that, Eagle 57 grew up in the world of chickens and learned everything about chickens. Language, culture, even economics and political issues of chickens. Eagle 57 studied so hard. A poem took an ordinary chicken a few years to learn by heart, but he memorized it in just a few weeks.

The poem was: "Being a chick, don't dare to fly, run round the mill, make a big thigh, then together, meet the butcher!"

At that time, Eagle 57 didn't know what a butcher was. He only knew to follow the chickens wherever they went and did whatever they did.

In the morning, Eagle 57 gargled with pebbles. It hurt his mouth, but he tried so hard because he was a potential chicken! In the afternoon, Eagle 57 hunted for worms in the garden. It hurt his beak, but he tried so hard because he was a potential chicken!

Besides, his parents taught him to stay away from eagles. Eagle 57 remembered this lesson carefully, but he never had a chance to practice it. Life just went on peacefully.

One day, the chickens were eating rice in the garden. Suddenly, a chicken looked up to the sky and rolled his eyes.

"Eagle!"

After that chicken screamed, all of them fled in disorder, except Eagle 57. He stood there, watching the eagle. In size, it looked like a giant flying black chicken with enormous wings that could cover the sun. The chickens were frightened, but Eagle 57 was too excited to be scared, he wanted to fly like that!

The eagle hovered over the chicken farm for a while, then suddenly changed direction. It swooped down to the position of Eagle 57. He shivered a little but stood still to watch the eagle's majesty. It raised two sharp claws, ready to catch Eagle 57.

WHOOSH!!!

Eagle 57 found himself lying in a bush. It turned out that his chicken dad had just rushed out to save him from the eagle.

"Are you crazy?" shouted his father. "Stay away from the eagle. Are you clear?"

Eagle 57 nodded. A few days later, that eagle appeared from time to time, but he just hid in a bush. Eagle 57 looked at it, wishing someday he could fly over the fences, rising above the tree, traveling to the mountain in the distance.

On his birthday, Eagle 57 was given a book titled *Keep Dreaming, Keep Going*, written by Mouse 92, a new emerging singer. Reading it made him very excited. Although Eagle 57 was quiet and had no sense of humor, he made his whole chicken family laugh out loud by saying that he intended to practice flying. Then the chickens got together and sang the familiar poem.

Eagle 57 was upset, but a line from Mouse 92's book encouraged him: "Every dream was a joke until someone achieved it."

The next day, Eagle 57 was determined to prove everyone wrong. He climbed onto the roof of the chicken coop and raised his potential wings. The chickens gathered around and tried to stop him.

"Oh my goodness!" the chicken mom exclaimed. "My son, if you had a crush on a girl and it ended, or you're lacking money, please tell me. Don't do that!"

Ignoring everyone, Eagle 57 had a strong belief: He can fly! He took a deep breath in, then jumped down.

THUD!!!

The fall made Eagle 57 pass out. The only one thing he remembered was a big cracking sound when his body landed.

When he woke up in the hospital, Eagle 57 found himself with a thick cast on his broken arm. Somewhere out there, the chicks were singing together: "A naive chick tried to fly. Broke his arm, went to the doc. From now on, no more flying..."

Watching the chicken dad regretfully hand a huge bag of money to the doctor, Eagle 57 was very sad. He promised to himself that from now on, he would be obedient to his parents, so they wouldn't have to waste money.

Later, Eagle 57 was fully recovered and went home. The first thing he did was to bury the book by Mouse 92 near the stream bank, and accepted his fate to be a chicken. His goal was to become the most potential chicken.

The 18th birthday of Eagle 57 was also the day he completed many difficult exams, including speed eating rice, running around the mill like crazy, and chewing pebbles. On the day of the exam score release, the whole chicken village gathered around Eagle 57's house to celebrate. He was the valedictorian.

"Great!" the chicken dad exclaimed. "You have made our family proud!"

"That's more than awesome!" the chicken mom exclaimed. "You've been recruited directly by the K.F.C. Few people could be there."

Eagle 57 was thrilled. Everyone congratulated him, except his grandfather, standing silently in the corner. His tears fell on the ground.

It was not until the afternoon, Eagle 57 went to his grandfather and asked, "Grandpa, why did you cry this morning?"

Tears in his eyes, the chicken grandpa said, "You are so wonderful, I don't want to lose you. There is one truth you should know. The butcher is someone who works in a slaughterhouse, and it's not a nice place. The humans didn't want to upset the chickens, so they lied to them."

Eagle 57 was startled. He had a hunch that something was not right. He listened to his grandfather carefully.

"There are... sharp knives. In a few minutes, your legs, your wings, your butt, each of them will be in a different place."

"That means..." Eagle 57 opened his mouth widely. "That means being killed?"

The chicken grandpa nodded. "You are so smart. It took a whole day for me to explain that to the last valedictorian chickens. They couldn't understand why each of their limbs would be in different places. They thought of some cloning magic."

Eagle 57 was shocked as if a bolt of lightning struck him. After years of hard work to become the most potential chicken, he finally understood what a butcher was. If he knew this earlier, he would let the old eagle catch and eat him on the mountain. At least, he could fly in the sky for a while.

"Don't worry," said the chicken grandpa, patting Eagle 57's shoulders. "Everyone will die in the end. Being the valedictorian and meeting the butcher should make you proud. You should go to the stream's bank and look at yourself for the last time. This afternoon, the K.F.C. truck will come to pick you up."

Eagle 57 wandered away. It was the second time he went to the stream bank. The last one was to bury the inspiring book, and this one was to hide his sadness.

At the stream bank, looking into the water, he was shocked. His image was the same as the mighty eagle flying in the sky in the old days. Perhaps back then, due to concentrating on burying the book, he didn't notice.

Eagle 57 felt like he had an electric shock. The eagle's heart kept thumping. The eagle's blood in his veins boiled. Eagle 57 rushed home and quickly jumped to the top of the tallest chicken coop.

A cool breeze blew through his wings. Eagle 57 was more excited than ever. This time he would fly! He definitely could get out of here!

As usual, the chicken family gathered around to try to stop him.

"My son!" the chicken dad shouted. "The door of K.F.C. is waiting open for you. Don't do anything foolish!"

"My son!" the chicken mom exclaimed. "I love you so much. How can I live without you?"

The chicken grandpa stood there, smiling.

Tears raced down both of his cheeks; Eagle 57 was determined to fly. He stepped backward to gain momentum. Spreading his wings, he started to run. He had never run so fast. Perhaps years of running around the mill made his legs stronger. When getting to the edge, he jumped and tried to flap his wings.

"It's unbelievable," Eagle 57 thought. "I'm flying!"

His eyes welled with tears of joy. Eagle 57 flew over the fence that held him back for years. When flying across the old stream, he saw his reflection in the water. A surge of excitement made him believe: Chickens can evolve into eagles!

The faraway mountain was more and more visible before his sharp-sighted eyes. A strong wind made him wobble. He swung his wings to fight back, but the wind was tougher than he thought. Perhaps years of training legs made his wings weak.

Eagle 57 found himself falling very fast!

THUD!!!!

Later, the only thing Eagle 57 could remember was he crashed into the K.F.C. truck, which was on its way to the chicken farm. The old wound throbbing made him faint.

Waking up, Eagle 57 found himself in a house, and he could see the high mountain through the windows. As soon as his feet touched the ground, someone rushed in and hugged him.

That was his birth mother, also the same mighty eagle in the sky before. His mom always watched him and saved him from the K.F.C. truck. She said something, but he did not understand. Eagle 57 realized a big problem: He did not know his native language!

To fit in the eagle society, he must overcome a difficult test, including re-learning the eagle's language and studying the eagles' economic and political issues. Thanks to his built-in qualities, Eagle 57 learned very quickly.

Because his wings were so weak, his mom made him practice karate-chopping wood every day. The feeling of breaking each piece of wood was terrible, but he was determined to overcome it. The next level was chopping the bricks. After that, Eagle 57's wings were extremely strong. Next, he learned to fly again, but the eagle's flight exercise was not jumping from the top of the chicken coop but the top of the mountain.

Eagle 57 was scared initially, but later, he got through and even won the gold medal in *flying through storms* at the Olympic games. Now, he could easily fly everywhere.

Later, people nominated him as the mayor of Eagle City. Eagle 57 came up with a crazy idea that discouraged his whole eagle family: Open free flight classes for chickens.

When interviewed about the purpose of his futuristic idea, Eagle 57 said:

"Some people thought that idea would make chickens become fatter prey in the sky, thanks to their slowness. That's not true. I aim to make the chickens believe in themselves and be able to enjoy the vast sky. I haven't eaten meat for years, and I'm still thriving. Eagles only need to eat rice to be healthy."

After that announcement, Eagle 57 opened KFChay, the most famous vegan restaurant chain. He taught me a profound lesson about belief: The only limitation is the limitation we put on ourselves.

Besides, his terrible fall when trying to fly taught me a lesson about training: Strong belief might give you strong motivation, but if you don't practice regularly to improve your skills, you'll always depend on luck.

10

Chicken 10
Every Issue Has Three Sides

Which came first, the chicken or the egg?

That question had troubled many Numagician philosophers. The world was divided into two factions, fighting each other to protect their opinions. One side believed that the chicken came first because chickens laid eggs. The other objected because eggs hatched chickens.

This question was a hot issue discussed for many years at the H.A.N. summit, including humans (H,) animals (A,) and numbers (N.) At each conference, there was a long table. On one side of the table was a chick about to lay an egg; the other side lay an about-to-hatch egg. When the discussion was going nowhere, they would wait to see if the chicken laid first or the egg hatched first, then claim their temporary victory.

On that day, people chose the egg containing Chicken 10. At the moment when two sides were most stressed out, Chicken 10 kicked off his eggshell. If previous chickens hatched and saw a rioting crowd, they would be afraid and run away. Chicken 10 was very different.

The moment Chicken 10 was born, he took 10 steps, stood still, looked up into the sky, and said as if he was a prophet: "Does the egg or chicken come first? It depends on whether that chicken is a rooster or a hen!"

The whole audience laughed.

"Hey chick," said one person from the chicken-first side. "Which came first, the hen or the egg?"

"Dear sir," answered Chicken 10 confidently. "It depends on whether that hen is infertile or not."

The whole audience nodded.

"Hey chick," asked one person from the egg-first side. "Assuming that is a perfectly healthy hen, then which will come first? The healthy hen or the egg?"

"Dear sir," Chicken 10 said. "In my opinion, it depends on whether the egg is a chicken egg or a duck egg?"

The whole audience clapped.

"Hey chick," said the referee. "Let's say it's a 100% chicken egg, and it will surely hatch. Which will come first?"

Chicken 10 was silent for a while. Finally, he asked, "How can the answer to that question benefit the world?"

The whole audience was silent.

Nobody ever thought about it. Assuming that one of the factions won this debate, what benefits were there for the world? Perhaps the only advantage was that the winning side could enjoy their victory and laugh at the other's defeat.

Later, Chicken 10 jumped off the table. He walked out the door and ran towards the chicken farm in the distance. After he was gone, the hen on the table laid an egg, but nobody cared.

This time the egg-first side won, but nobody was excited. It was also the last H.A.N. conference discussing this issue. At future conferences, people focused on more practical matters, including preventing people from hunting rare species in the red book and stopping animals in the black book from destroying the crops.

As for Chicken 10, he didn't remember anything in that conference, as if God had manipulated him. That made sense because no baby chicken could debate as good as that!

Later, Chicken 10 became a wise consultant who could always see things that no one had seen before. Many people in Numagician came to him for advice. His famous quote was, "Everyone can see two sides of a problem, but when you find the third side, the problem will be solved by itself."

Eagle 57, the KFChay restaurant owner, once personally visited Chicken 10 with his son and talked about his overweight problem.

"Hey boy," Chicken 10 asked the young eagle. "The high sky is the desire of all species. Don't you want to fly up there?"

With sadness in his eyes, the young eagle said. "Yes. But because I was too fat, I failed the flight exam in primary school."

"Why don't you stop eating to lose weight?"

"The food is too delicious, and I want to eat as much as I can."

"Why don't you eat food that is not delicious?"

"Your question is strange. How can I eat tasteless food?"

"Okay, so in your mind, you have only two kinds of food. Delicious and not delicious food. Is that right?"

"Yes. I will eat delicious food, and I won't eat tasteless food."

"Do you want to try the third kind of food?"

The young eagle thought for a while, then he replied, " Okay."

Chicken 10 ran into the kitchen, slowly brought out a bowl containing something small and white. "Try this food and tell me if it is delicious or not."

The young eagle poured the food into his mouth and chewed quickly. "It's not delicious."

"You are eating so fast," Chicken 10 said. "While chewing, please count from 1 to 10, then swallow."

This time, the young eagle chewed 10 times. After he swallowed, his eyes opened widely, "Wow, it's so sweet! What is this?"

"That's cooked rice," said Chicken 10. "It's an invention of Rabbit 28. The more you chew, the more delicious it will be!"

After that conversation, Eagle 57 decided to put cooked rice on the menu of his restaurant. That was a miracle! After only a few months, the young eagle was no longer fat, and he began to fly one foot up in the air for the first time.

Just like that, Chicken 10 helped many people, including Lion 51. Although Lion 51 roared, his son used the smartphone all day. At first, Lion 51 thought that his roar was not loud enough, so he went to the mountain to train his voice. When he got back, he could roar louder than his older brother in the past. But in the end, he still used his smartphone a lot, and his vision was failing.

Chicken 10 listened to Lion 51's story carefully, then he said, "Do you know what your kid does with the smartphone?"

"Oh..." Lion 51 said. "I saw something jump up and shoot the hunters."

"Ah, it's a video game."

"So how can I make my son stop? He is the first lion who has short-sighted eyes in our whole lion family!"

"What do you think playing video games will help your son achieve?"

"I see no benefit at all. Except for the happy expression on my son's face every time he plays!"

"Why was he so excited?"

"He roared when he defeated some hunters."

"Why did he want to defeat those hunters?"

"Well, could it be that he wanted the feeling of victory like his grandpa in the past?"

"We are going in the right direction. Why did your son want to be like his grandpa?"

"He wanted to be respectful and be loved by everyone?"

"Exactly!" Chicken 10 smiled. "When your son played video games, you only saw two sides: First, your son was excited. Second, you suffered. Now you see the third side: Your son needs attention."

Lion 51 was startled, his tears welled up. "I see, yet I roared as if he was bad. That was a waste of months training my voice so hard on the mountain."

Since that day, Lion 51 hadn't roared at his son anymore. He even played video games with him. Later, he asked his son to talk to people, training his social skills like grandpa.

Every problem has more than two sides, and when you find the third side, the problem will be solved by itself.

Monkey 37
When Birds Dig And Fish Fly.

Can you guess who will get the most benefit from a contest? Is it the contestant who can be famous after that? Is it the spectator who can enjoy the thrilling show? In my opinion, it's the organizer who sold tickets. Monkey 37 is the best event manager I've ever known.

I knew Monkey 37 in a banana picking contest when he was just a sweeper, collecting extra bananas on the ground after each game. Several years later, he became an event manager with a salary of up to a million Susu.

Monkey 37 told me that the contests went very well in the past, and the tickets sold out within a week. But later, the games became boring, and the sales started to decline. The organizers had a lot of difficulties.

At that time, the 37 Monkey had many strange ideas. For example, a fish must swim upstream, an eagle must fly into the storms, or an elephant must run fast on the edge of the wall. The organizers rejected those ideas because they were too risky.

The 37 Monkey did not give up. He improved an old contest to build the confidence of the organizers. That was the traditional banana picking contest. After picking a banana and peeling it, the monkeys must throw the banana peel into the trash and feed the banana to the audience.

Surprisingly, the sales increased dramatically. The contest was successful beyond expectation. After that, they researched the audience. The reason was everyone wanted to eat free bananas without peeling or throwing the banana peels into the trash.

After that, one by one, the 37 Monkey made his ideas come true. Thanks to them, he got rich quickly and became the head of the organizing committee. To celebrate, the 37 Monkey decided to hold a unique contest. If the previous games were for only one particular species, he wanted more species to appear in one contest.

I got an invitation letter to join a triathlon: Flying, swimming, and digging. Participants were anyone who believed that they were fish, birds, or worms. The contest rules were also very simple. Candidates would have to join three games, then compare the overall scores. That means if I join the game, a bird like me must not only fly but also swim and dig.

Speaking of flying, the fastest flight I've ever made was when a dog chased me. Not to mention those two other challenging games. At first, I would not join, but the prize was so big, up to one million Susus. I couldn't resist the temptation. Not only me, but Monkey 37 had also sent invitations to every bird, fish, and worm in the area.

The contest was very intriguing, and the tickets sold out in just one day which urged the organizers to print more. The atmosphere of the competition stirred all over Numagician. Since the day they launched the contest, the mouse singing voice in my forest had been gone. Instead, people could hear the sound of something hitting the ground all day. That was because the birds were training their beaks. My neighbor's house collapsed because the owner trained his beak so hard while digging, so he destroyed its foundation.

I found myself very lucky because I didn't live near the river bank. People there had trouble sleeping because of the sound of something dropping into the water all day. The fish were training to fly. Many of them went to the hospital due to jumping too high, which led to a lack of oxygen.

The contest hadn't taken place yet, but it created a significant disturbance in Numagician daily activities. After breaking their beaks due to digging training, many birds changed their plans to practice swimming in the hope of raising the overall scores. As a result, they broke their wings, too. After digging so hard, many fish broke their fins and went to the hospital. Strangely, the hospital reports showed there were many fish and birds, but no worms!

Perhaps they were too afraid to join?

No way, I saw many worms digging very hard near my house. Regardless, I had to practice, too. There were three games, but I was not good at any. I wonder which one I should practice first.

Finally, the contest day came. I fully packed a suitcase but just went to watch it. Over the past few months, I had been too lazy; watching others practicing made me forget my training. I ended up having to pay hundreds of Susu to buy a ticket to see the contest.

They held the contest in the territory of the eagles. The stadium was a vast alley with the capacity of hundreds of thousands of species. Animals, numbers, and humans, everyone gathered there. It looked like the organizers had made a lot of money.

"Hi, everyone!" Monkey 37 spoke through a microphone. "Someone asked me why I held this strange contest. My answer is, why not?"

The whole crowd was excited.

"Over the years, we have held many great competitions. Most of them were for powerful species like elephants, lions, and eagles. What about birds, fish, and worms? They were the spectators most of the time and contributed a lot through buying tickets!"

The whole crowd laughed.

"I want to hold this contest. First of all, I want to pay tribute to them. And then, I want to tell the world that anyone can compete!"

The whole crowd clapped their hands. The excitement appeared on the candidates' faces. When they shot the beginning signal, the triathlon officially started.

In the qualifying rounds, each species competed by their strengths. Birds competed in flying, fish in swimming, and worms in digging. After that, the organizers would choose one of the best contestants, representing each species to compete in the final round.

Before the final round, the three contestants had a few days of training to improve their skills. The fish practiced flying very hard, which led him to lack oxygen, and he went to the hospital for recovery. Therefore, in the final, there was only the bird and the worm. However, the bird had practiced swimming hard too, so one of his wings was bandaged.

As a result, the bird got only 7/10 points at flying and 2/10 at swimming, and he quit digging from the beginning. The overall score for the bird was 9/30. As for the worm, he refused to join two other games and just dug and got the store for 10/10. Finally, the worm won with an overall score of 10/30.

The audience was outraged because the contestants didn't participate in the games that were not their talents, especially the worm. While the organizers were presenting the trophies, the audience threw slippers and tomatoes at them and asked for a refund.

"I know you are very upset," said Monkey 37, calmly. "You've paid hundreds of Susu expecting to see a flying worm, a swimming bird, and a fish that can dig."

The crowd calmed down. Perhaps Monkey 37 had spoken to the audience's hearts.

"I know we didn't meet your expectations. But look at what we've got here. At least you saw a three-in-one contest, and our three contestants had performed extremely well in the qualifying rounds before they got to the final."

The whole crowd nodded.

"They also taught us a precious lesson. This worm won because he focused only on his talent and got the highest score, which is very rare in the worm family. Therefore, if your life is too hard, maybe you are trying to be someone else, not yourself. The worm reminded us of a lesson: Focus on your talent, then you will be a champion!"

The whole crowd stood up and clapped their hands continuously. In the end, everyone was happy because of the lesson they learned for themselves. I also went home to reflect seriously on my talent.

I was reminded of a memory when I was in kindergarten. At lunchtime, the teacher asked each of us to show some talent. I didn't know what to do, so I told a story. I don't remember what I said at that time, but the whole class laughed loudly. When I got home, my mom said that my talent was storytelling.

After that, I took a pen and wrote about everything that had happened in that contest, then sent it to Monkey 37.

The next day, I received a reply from Monkey 37. "Hey, I was very impressed with your report. I want to invite you to be our reporter. It's a long-term job with an irresistible salary. What do you think?"

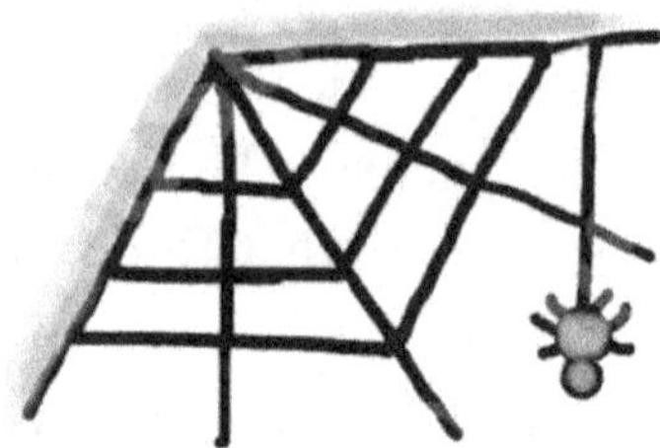

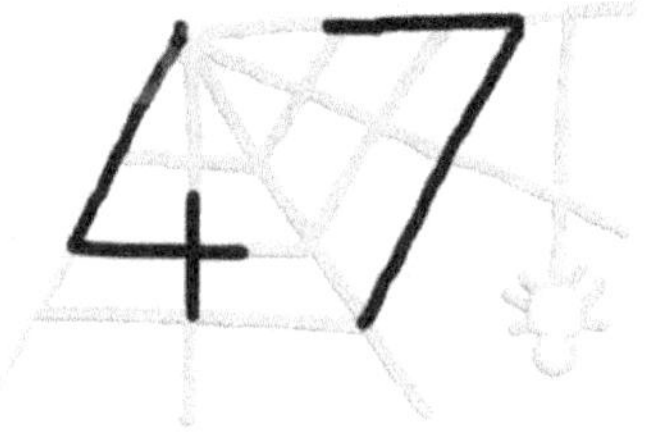

Spider 47
Are Spiders Lazy Or Not?

In your opinion, is laziness good or bad? Before I met Spider 47, I always thought that laziness was terrible. Little did I know that there was an exciting kind of laziness: smart laziness.

When Rabbit 28 returned to Numagician, I helped her clean the lab full of spider webs. That was the moment I saw Spider 47.

At first glance, you might think that spiders are hard-working. Wherever people forget to clean, the spiders will show up and make their webs. Spider 47 said, "Actually, the spiders in the old days were truly hard workers, but my grandpa made them lazy as you see today."

In the dawn of time, while creating animals, God inscribed some instructions on using their talents in their brains. Perhaps because there were too many species, so he forgot the spiders. Therefore, the spiders felt that their silks were so annoying and didn't use them, except for tying up the prey.

At that time, the spider family had a prophecy that said you would fly if you ate animals that had wings. Therefore, the favorite dish of the spiders was the flies, but they were too fast. To catch flies, the spiders must stalk them day and night, wait for the perfect moment to rush in, tie them by silks, and then carry them back to the cave.

That would be the sole use of spider silk if Spider 47's grandpa were not born. He refused to hunt the flies but just ate the food everyone brought home. When being asked, he said, "I'm wondering if there is a faster way to catch the flies."

Although everybody criticized Spider 47's grandpa for being lazy, they loved him. Because he wasn't spending a lot of time hunting, Grandpa was able to come up with many ideas that amused everyone. Sometimes he used spider silk to jump from branch to branch like Spiderman. Other times he created funny sounds by plucking a string made from spider silks. The most exciting idea was to make a ball from spider silks, then ask everyone to kick it everywhere. He invented spider football!

One day, something happened while he was making a net from spider silks to play a new sport called volleyball. When he sketched the net to test the durability, a flock of flies passed by and stuck there. That night, the whole spider family had a big party, everyone was full without doing any work. He discovered a new use of spider silk: the spider web.

Later, a great revolution called *spider web* made spiders lazier than ever. Every evening, the spiders weaved the nets. Every morning, they spread their nets where insects often passed by. Every afternoon, they leisurely went to see the results. Some spiders were so lazy that they ate the prey on the spot, then they wrapped the leftovers with the silks to save it for the next day. Another use of spider silk was invented: to preserve the food.

"Is there a faster way?" is a great question. Not only did it help Spider 47's grandpa have something to think of, but it also brought many excellent ideas. That question had been passed down from generation to generation among spiders.

Spider 47 knew the power of this special question very well. When Monkey 37 used pigeons to send invitation letters to all the animals, Spider 47 asked, "Is there a faster way to deliver the letters?"

Later, he made lots of money by inventing *The Spider Network*. The basic idea is to connect every house with spider silks. When you need to send a letter, vibrate the spider silk at your home, then a spider mail carrier will show up to collect your letter. We call them the spider mail carriers.

At first, the spider mail carrier jumped from your house to the address on the envelope. It took a lot of time to do so. Spider 47 asked the question again, "Is there a faster way?"

One idea came up, which was to use the transit stations. Spider 47 recruited many spider mail carriers and set up transit mail stations everywhere. Thanks to that, they wouldn't have to travel to the recipients' address. They just brought the mail to the nearest transit mail station and let other spider mail carriers continue the delivery. This way not only saved money, but also created more jobs for the spider family. Besides, the spider network project also helped the pigeons to retire early.

There was only one annoying issue. Because silks were spread everywhere, the rate of insects caught in the spider web multiplied each year. This issue got Eagle 57's attention. After his successful campaign *Eagle Eat Rice* to protect the chickens, he also had a concern about the insects. They discussed this problem at the H.A.N. conference last year; the spider network project might need to be stopped.

Once again, the spider family's usual question saved Spider 47's project from failure. Thanks to always being optimistic about whether there was a faster way, he came up with a new idea: The electronic spider network. He replaced the spider silk in the spider network with a slippery material that no insect couldn't be stuck in. That material also had a remarkable ability to connect with personal computers invented by Rabbit 28.

That meant if you owned a personal computer connected to the electronic spider network, you could freely chat with your loved ones thousands of feet away from you. When I came to your world, I was surprised that you also have this system called the Internet!

In his speech to introduce the system, Spider 47 called himself a smart lazy man. He said one thing that made me remember forever: "What if there were no lazy people in this world? There would be no great invention that helped us save more time. Sometimes, laziness is a quality of a genius."

Please note that there are two kinds of laziness: ordinary laziness and smart laziness. Ordinary lazy people would spend much of their time sleeping and entertaining. As for smart lazy people, they allow themselves to relax but always ask: Is there a faster way? You can try that, too!

Snail 26
Come To The Top, See The Sky!

When you get to know a new exciting friend, it's typical to be happy. When I got acquainted with Snail 26, I was in terrible pain!

Please don't get me wrong. Actually, Snail 26 is very kind. Only the kids in the mountain near his house are bad. That time while flying around to see the clouds as white as cotton candy there was a bang. I fell down like a jackfruit falling and passed out.

Waking up, I found myself lying on a large leaf with one wing bandaged. I immediately stood up and had a severe throbbing pain.

"Please don't move..."

That voice came from a giant snail, looking at me with kind eyes. It was Snail 26 who saved me from the hands of human kids.

It would be difficult to tell if Snail 26 was a male or a female from its appearance. When asked, Snail 26 didn't understand what gender was. Well, it doesn't matter, the most important thing is I got a new great friend!

Have you ever given up or been accused of doing things halfway?

I used to have that bad habit, but my time staying with Snail 26 has changed me. All it took was to follow him to pick medicinal plants on the mountaintop.

Honestly, I had flown to thousands of mountaintops, and I never thought that one day I would have to climb a mountain with my chopstick-like legs.

How miserable!

Not to mention that Snail 26 moved terribly slow. Sometimes I thought perhaps my wings would be healed entirely before using herbal medicine. Although I was impatient, I did not dare go ahead for fear of getting lost.

How miserable!

Many times I blamed myself for choosing the wrong place to fly around. I flew to the exact location where the H.A.N. peace treaty had not been signed. That enabled the kids to shoot me. Sometimes when I saw them, my wings throbbed.

How miserable!

There was a strange thing that happened. In suffering, I could feel joy. Maybe I am used to flying fast, so the only thing I've seen was the trees' green color. I didn't notice that they might look alike, but each tree had its own interesting features.

Many trees had big trunks, but they all fell after a strong wind blew by. Other trees might be tiny, but they stayed in the ground. Snail 26 explained that the big trees focused on growing their trunks and never took care of their roots. The small trees' roots were often ten times longer than their bodies, enabling them to stand firm in the soil.

There was something else. I was used to drinking so fast that I did not enjoy water. Snail 26 showed me an exciting way to make water strangely delicious.

When Snail 26 saw a cloud of fog floating by, he smiled and put a large leaf on his head. I did as he did. It turned out that later we got water droplets on it.

According to Snail 26, we have the most nutritious water of all time with a beautiful name: Dew on the Leaf.

"Hey, Snail 26. I feel good, but it's not enough!"

"Hey, Bird 69. What is your purpose for drinking water? You drink a lot to go to the bathroom or to provide enough water for the body?"

After that, Snail 26 explained that our body needs a sufficient amount of water. The most important thing was the way we drink. Then he showed me the way snails drink with super clear steps.

First, you have to adjust the leaf to separate a small drop of water from the big dew. Next, you open your mouth, raise the leaf and make sure that the droplet would fall on your tongue, not in your nostrils.

I had to work very hard to do this as slowly and perfectly as Snail 26. When a droplet touched my tongue and melted in my mouth, I felt that it was the sweetest water in the world.

Just like that, sometimes we stopped to drink a drop of water. It was weird but also miraculous. Although I drank less than usual, I wasn't thirsty, and the water was better than ever.

We made it to the mountaintop in no time. The clear sky appeared before my eyes. Perhaps for many years looking into the sky while flying, I didn't know how interesting it looked from the ground. Maybe I made an effort to climb the mountain, which led to that good feeling.

"Hey, Snail 26. Why can't I see any kids up here?"

"Bird 69, no kid has ever reached a mountaintop. Every time they got close to the top and saw a foggy cloud, they went down and climbed another mountain that wasn't surrounded by clouds. When they found a new mountain, the clouds reappeared. They tried again. That's why they never reached the top."

Just as Snail 26 said, we found the kids arguing while going down after picking the medicinal herbs. One kid complained that there was too much fog and suggested searching for another mountain with clearer vision. They did that.

"When you are already on a mountain, don't look for another mountain." That was what my mom told me. Now I could see it with my own eyes. Those kids would never see the blue sky like us if they always refused to go through the foggy clouds.

"Climb at least one mountaintop. You will see the whole sky!" Snail 26 told me when we said goodbye to each other.

Later, I spent one week at home, waiting for my wings to heal. I thought a lot about that idea. I wrote down the unfinished tasks in the past and began to complete them one by one. The feeling of achieving something that I had started was incredible.

Moreover, every time I was in trouble, I remembered the foggy clouds and those kids right away. That motivated me to finish what I started.

Antelope 97
Which Seeds Will Germinate?

Has anyone ever complimented you on having a gorgeous elbow or the perfectly balanced position of your head on your shoulders?

Anyone who met Antelope 97 would be extremely happy because he could always find something good to praise.

I became acquainted with Antelope 97 while taking a walk with Rabbit 28. She was engrossed in the idea of automatic fire extinguishers, then stumbled upon a rock. Antelope 97 passed by and helped her stand up.

When Rabbit 28 found out that one of her teeth had been chipped, her eyes welled up with tears. The last time she cried, God gave her more time to live. This time she might cry louder, but he wouldn't restore her chipped tooth.

"Don't worry," Antelope 97 put his hands on her shoulders. "Thanks to this chipped tooth, the others look better."

Grinning, Rabbit 28 wiped her tears away. She continued walking and spoke passionately about a new idea: anti-chipped teeth. The praise of Antelope 97 was super powerful!

When we parted, he gave me a business card. It turned out that Antelope 97 was a teacher. He taught a strange subject which stimulated my curiosity by its name: You are Gorgeous.

The next day, I had to call Antelope 97. I really wanted to know how my shaggy fur could be gorgeous?

As instructed, I found his class in a giant banana garden at the end of the forest. The desks were made from giant banana stumps, and on each desk was a shiny mirror. Including me, the class had 97 students. Everyone was excited, waiting for Antelope 97. Finally, he walked out onto the stage holding something in his hands.

"There are two seeds in my hands," Antelope 97 said. "One is a new big fresh banana seed, I call it the good one. The other is an old flat dried pomelo seed, let's call it the bad one. Which one do you think will grow into a tree?"

A spider raised his legs and replied, "The big banana seed will do!"

Antelope 97 put the banana seed in his pocket, then threw the pomelo to the ground. "The one you sow will do."

The whole class nodded, except for a monkey scratching his head and ears. Finally, he asked, "What if we sow both? The big banana seed will definitely grow!"

Antelope 97 took the banana seed from his pocket and threw it to the ground. Next, he took a bucket of water and only watered the pomelo seed. "When you sow both of them, the one that gets water will grow!"

The whole class nodded again, except for a lion. He roared, "If we sow and water both of them, the big banana seed will grow for sure, not the small pomelo seed!"

Antelope 97 smiled, then he took several sticks of wood nearby to make a fence around the pomelo seed. "Even so, the one you protect will grow."

The class fell silent, waiting for the explanation from Antelope 97.

"Each of us is like a seed. It doesn't matter whether it's good or bad for it to grow. The compliment is like the water, helping the seed grow. Now I want you to look in the mirror in front of you then say aloud: I'm beautiful when being myself."

Am I beautiful? That was the most ridiculous thing I ever did. Although I was a bit shy, I did the same when the whole class said it in unison. It's said that a thousand lies would become true. After reading that sentence a thousand times, I began to feel that I wasn't as bad as I thought. However, we didn't know how to be ourselves, so Antelope 97 explained it with a story.

Once upon a time, there were two gardens—one big, one small. The big garden had several small pomelo trees. In the small garden, there was only one large banana tree. It was that big, thanks to the special care of its master, a boy.

The boy not only watered it regularly but also protected it from bad weather. On hot summer days, he opened the window to let the air out from his room to cool the whole garden. On cold winter days, he used cotton blankets to cover the trees. Thanks to him, the banana tree was always happy and green.

When the girl next door moved in, the banana tree was thrilled. She talked to it every day. Many times she confided in the banana tree until midnight and fell asleep under it. Thanks to her, the banana tree became overgrown.

In the harvest season, it produced large bunches of bananas. Each banana was big like an ear of corn and had a bright yellow color, with a fragrant smell. Everyone, including the villagers and the evil monkeys wanted to visit the garden and brought home several banana bunches. Thanks to them, the small garden was always crowded.

One day, while watering in the small garden, the boy heard thud sounds. He immediately ran to the big garden and took a look. The banana tree waited, but the boy didn't come back. It tried its best to look over the fence to see what happened.

In the big garden, under the small pomelo trees, there were countless big pomelos. Watching the boy and the neighbor girl enjoying each piece of delicious pomelo, the banana was a little sad. It thought, "The boy will come back."

Life is not as sweet as a dream. Over time, the pomelo garden became more and more prosperous. The boy and the girl fell in love with the pomelos. On stormy days, they built fences to protect the pomelo trees. On cold days, they had a bonfire party under the pomelo trees. They forgot about the banana tree.

In the harvest season, the banana tree still produced large bunches of bananas. Each banana was big like an ear of corn and had a bright yellow color, with a fragrant smell. However, no one cared about them. Perhaps they were attracted by the thud sounds of pomelos falling in the nearby garden.

It was just like that from season to season. The banana tree didn't know what to do except to sadly watch its golden bunches of bananas stolen by the evil monkeys, or lying rotten on the ground.

One day, the banana tree came up with a great idea. I thought, "What if I could produce a pomelo that is two times bigger than every usual pomelo in the big garden? People will come back, and the evil monkeys will leave. I'll be happy!"

In order to produce big pomelos, the banana tree decided to stop making any fruit in the next harvest season, to devote all its strength to the last season. Season after season, the banana tree spent all nutrients received from mother nature on this great purpose.

Time had passed. Finally, the big day had come. The banana tree had many bunches of big pomelos after many seasons of fruitlessness. From a distance of hundreds of yards, people could see them dangling on the banana tree. The news spread, and everybody poured into the old small garden, including the evil monkeys, the boy, and the neighbor girl. Everybody was happy.

The banana tree was thrilled. It thought, "God has eyes. Its efforts have paid off."

The banana tree shook itself, and a big bunch of pomelos fell. When it landed, there was no thud sound, but a splat sound. Some pomelos on the ground were crushed. The boy picked up one piece of pomelo and ate it.

"Oh man," the boy spat it out. "It tasted like a banana!"

The whole crowd was upset. Suddenly, they heard the thud sounds coming from the big garden. They went there to eat real pomelos.

The evil monkeys stayed, discussing whether they should try the pomelo from the banana tree or not.

Finally, the monkey leader picked up a piece of pomelo off the ground and ate it.

"That's good," it said to the monkeys, "But this banana tree was genetically modified. What kind of banana wears a pomelo's appearance? We should leave now."

The monkeys were dismissed and never came back.

Now there was only the big banana tree in the small garden. While looking at the vast sky, the banana tree realized its mistake. It wished over the years, if it kept producing the bananas, it still had the monkeys as friends. The banana tree slowly closed its eyes, slowly dying, and returned to mother nature.

After listening to the story of Antelope 97, everyone felt great pity for the fate of the banana tree. When they asked for the meaning of this story, Antelope 97 mildly explained:

"I called that story *The Law of Fruit*. If you were born a banana seed, then try to be the greatest banana tree. Don't waste your time on making weird pomelo. That's the meaning of being yourself. Always remember who you are and develop the good in you. That is the best way to help your seeds grow."

Later, Antelope 97 made the class work in pairs to praise each other. I was with a man with an eyepatch, and he had a strange name: Terapi (reverse of pirate.) I didn't know what to praise. Suddenly, I remembered the compliment that Antelope 97 gave to Rabbit 28.

I said, "Your patched eye makes the other eye look more bright and gorgeous!"

He was silent for a while, then burst into tears. I asked the reason, but he did not answer. Later, he wiped his tears and said, "Thank you so much. I've never received a compliment like that. You help me realize that my other eye is so beautiful."

The class went on with joy, laughter, and even happy tears. I was also delighted when I got praise from a black raven. "You have the most colorful fur in the world."

One month later, I received a letter from a mental hospital. The title read, "About the condition of Mr. Terapi."

I was sweaty. Did my compliment that day affect his illness?

It turned out that it was a thank-you letter. The doctors said that one-eyed man had autism, and they were unable to cure him. Thanks to my compliment, his illness improved. Now, he was well enough to be discharged from the hospital.

I was so happy. The power of praise was genuinely incredible. However, I did not compliment people much in the past.

Someone knocked on the door. It was Terapi. He came to thank me and invited me to join the competition held by Antelope 97: Anyone Can Praise. The rules were simple. Everyone would talk and give others as many compliments as possible. Whether it was a flattering or real compliment, as long as you made others happy, you were getting scores.

Although he insisted that I should participate in the contest, I refused because I never won a prize in any competitions. The idea of praising that eyepatch making his other eye better was from Antelope 97. Before leaving, he gave me a newly published book by Antelope 97: Ultimate Handbook of Praising.

In the end, I still went to that contest as a spectator. The reason was that they had a lucky draw, and I also wanted to promote my strength as a reporter.

The article was great, many people read it, and they were impressed by the compliments I had recorded from the contest.

"You have a better smile than you think. Just open your beak and laugh!"

"Your fur looks sexier than a delicious rainbow popsicle with chocolate sprinkles!"

"Your storytelling skills can make a zombie pop up from its grave and laugh happily!"

If you go to Numagician and attend a class of Antelope 97, how do you think you would be commended?

Dragon 25
The Sky Painter

Have you ever thought of a land where everyone was mute? Great! Perhaps people would have fewer arguments and live more peacefully!

Well, the reality was different. I had been there, in a kingdom named EIM (Everyone Is Mute.) Thanks to the lucky draw in the contest "Anyone Can Praise" of Antelope 97. I won the prize, which was a free travel ticket to this unique land.

In EIM, Everyone was born mute. They communicated with each other by boards and pens. If you went there without a board or pen, you were doomed like a tsunami hit land while you were sunbathing. I thought that a tsunami hit me while burying myself under the sand because I did not bring both of them!

Therefore, instead of being at the hotel at 2:00 p.m., I was hanging around a stationary store till 5:00 p.m. Although I tried every gesture with my wings, the storekeeper didn't understand that all I wanted was to test the pen before purchasing. Finally, he sent a message to 911. He told the police that a crazy bird was flapping its wings and preventing him from selling.

At that moment, Dragon 25 appeared. The way he showed up was not like a hero coming to explain everything to the storekeeper and save me. He got caught while trying to steal a box of crayons. Watching people scold him by writing bad words on the boards, I realized a fascinating thing: When someone scolds you, normally, you cover your ears, but here in the EIM kingdom, all you need to do is close your eyes.

Later, the police came and cuffed Dragon 25 by his neck. At the doorway, he turned around and did something that made me cry with happy tears.

He swore!

Swearing was terrible, and you shouldn't interact with bad people. Even knowing that I couldn't stop myself from running to the door and following Dragon 25, the only one person here that was not mute.

As a consequence, I also got caught by the police. The storekeeper didn't forget his duty to kill two birds with one stone. The police caught both a thief and a crazy bird with just a single message from him.

That was how I met Dragon 25!

They locked us in a tiny cell, and Dragon 25 alone took up two-thirds of the area. I was a tranquil bird, but for some reason, we talked all night. I told him stories about my hometown with many beautiful friends. He told me about his fierce childhood.

Dragon 25 had no concept of a close friend. He said, "At birth, every child here could speak normally. But because everybody around them communicates by boards and pens, they forget that ability when they grow up. That does not affect me because I'm an orphan and also have a hobby of self-talking."

"What frustrated you the most?" I asked.

"It was my classmates. They teased me because I'm autistic and I would often use gestures while talking. They didn't know that I couldn't afford to buy a board and pen."

"Oh, I understand that." There was a flashback in my mind, flapping my wings to explain to that storekeeper.

That was not the most challenging part of his teenage years. At the puberty stage, every dragon could breathe fire to express themselves, but he could only spit black ink. His ink could last for a very long time in the air, so each time he sneezed, he made everything go pitch dark. Dragon 25 was upset because he had more shameful nicknames, including a weird dragon, the octopus dragon, the most humiliating dragon that couldn't grill a chicken.

Later, an incident had turned a new page in his life book. That page was more tattered than the old one.

That time, a group of bullies beat Dragon 25 and spread his ink everywhere. Then, they blamed him and had Dragon 25 expelled from school. Wandering on the street, Dragon 25 found an old pen factory. Here, he made his living by selling his ink at a low price. He soon had to quit that job because of health issues.

Last month, Dragon 25 found an old board. He drew a picture of an octopus spitting ink and hung it on the door to warn everyone not to come near. Unexpectedly, someone offered to buy the painting, but they would have paid ten times more if the picture was in color. Dragon 25 did not have any money, so he *borrowed* a box of crayons at the stationery shop where I had gotten into trouble. Fate had brought us together.

"Hey, Bird 69. When we get out, what are you going to do first?"

"Oh, I'll return to my hometown right away and never use a free travel ticket again. What about you?"

Dragon 25 sighed. "Perhaps I would sell that black and white picture for a low price. I hope the merchant hasn't left the city yet."

"Hey, you two!"

The warden called them. He opened the cell and announced the good news. "You two have been bailed."

Surprisingly, there was a royal seal on the release document. It turned out that the merchant who asked for Dragon 25's picture was the king's emissary. When the king found out, he granted Dragon 25 a giant box of crayons and asked him to finish the job as soon as possible to celebrate the princess's 25th birthday.

After that, I decided not to return yet. Instead of the hotel, I went straight to Dragon 25's house and stayed there. Although it was a small shabby cave, I felt good. I could help Dragon 25 mix the colors and avoid any new trouble in this land.

The Dragon 25's life book had turned to a new page, which was the best. It was also fun to see my face on that page.

I did not know whether the princess's zodiac sign was dragon or octopus, but she loved the painting of Dragon 25 very much. Later, she offered him a new job in the royal family which was highly paid and did not require a degree. I wanted to try, but when she read the job description, I knew it was only for Dragon 25.

When the king gave a speech by writing on a small board, a painting team would rewrite his words on a larger board. That was quite costly and ineffective. The princess asked Dragon 25 to paint the king's words in the sky so that everyone could see them more clearly.

The king approved that breakthrough idea immediately, but the painting team objected because Dragon 25 could only create black and white paintings, which was not attractive to most spectators. The king gave us one week to find a way to upgrade the blank ink of Dragon 25 to a new colorful version.

We tried having Dragon 25 wear bags of watercolors, but it would make him fly slowly and not follow the king's words. We also tried many other solutions, but they were not feasible. Three days before the deadline, I remembered Rabbit 28. In the past, except for the failure to create time, she never failed at anything.

So Dragon 25 flew me to Numagician, to meet with Rabbit 28. My hunch was right. After just one day of research, she created a color filter that looked like a large dog muzzle. It helped Dragon 25 to spit ink in any color he wanted by just thinking!

That was amazing!

On the princess's 25th birthday, the entire population in EIM saw a fantastic performance. Flying in the sky, Dragon 25 illustrated every word said by the king more vividly and perfectly than ever. Dragon 25 made everyone open their mouth widely to utter something after years of muting. Of course, I also made a little bit of money by writing an article for the royal newspaper.

A long time later, Dragon 25 still wrote me letters. He is now wealthy and even has an orphanage for raising kids with special needs like him. Most recently, Dragon 25 opened a class to teach adult people to speak again, with the hope of unmuting all people in EIM.

I learned from Dragon 25 one thing: No matter who or what you are, you will always have a unique talent waiting to be discovered.

Sheep 93
Born To Hug

"The two most important days in your life are the day you are born, and the day you find out why."

That idea of Mark Twain, a famous writer in your world, made me spend a lot of time on self-reflection with the questions: Who am I? Why was I born?

I saw that everybody here would ask that question at least once at some point in their lives. If you came to Numagician and asked those same questions, people would put you into a mental hospital until you remembered who you were.

Our God loves us so much that he created each number in Numagician an ID card, helping them remember who they are. Of course, there were exceptions. Several times he got too busy and forgot to instruct some numbers. One of them was Sheep 93. Not only Sheep 93, but all sheep in Numagician didn't know their purpose in life.

When humans showed up and said every sheep was born to be sheared, they believed that! It's terrible! Plucking a single feather is painful for me, let alone all the feathers on my body. Despite that, the sheep still obeyed humans in exchange for a warm barn and three meals per day.

Sheep 93 grew up in a prestigious family. Humans trusted his father to be the chief propaganda officer. That meant he gave speeches everywhere to help sheep realize their noble mission: Born to be sheared. So it was essential to take care of your wool. You had to do this to soften your wool, and you had to do that to whiten it. In general, a sheep's life was only about wool, wool, and wool.

Having a purpose in life was good, but Sheep 93 was troubled with one thing. Although his father always preached that sheep should be sheared by humans, no human sheared his wool. Once following him to a lecture, Sheep 93 decided to ask the big question.

"Papa," Sheep 93 asked. "Why do you convince them to provide their wool for humanity, but no human comes to shear yours?

Papa smiled. "Oh, my boy. It is an adult issue. You will understand later."

"I'm already grown up, Papa. You must tell me now."

He said nothing but sighed. After that, he went up to the pulpit and set the crowd on fire with their noble mission. Sheep 93 stood behind the backdrop, helping his father control the presentation slides, listening in resentment. He couldn't help asking: Why were sheep born? What was he born for?

The questions kept burning in his heart and liver. Sheep 93 believed that his thick fur had a more meaningful purpose. It was nonsense to spend a lifetime taking care of something, then to let humans take it.

Sheep 93 also confided in some close friends, but his father had brainwashed them. The topics most concerned about were nothing but wool, wool, and wool. His mother, his aunts, and his cousins, all were the same. Unable to bear this loneliness, Sheep 93 decided to leave to find the answer.

However, his house was similar to a sheep palace, full of guards, operating 24/7. Not to mention, his father had buried plenty of plucking mines around the house. If you got one, it would remove your wool in seconds. Therefore, escaping was not easy. Sheep 93 had to plan very carefully, and the key was to steal the mine map in his father's office, which was seriously guarded.

Fortunately, his father got drunk with humans one day, so Sheep 93 was granted permission to bring him into his office alone. Taking that opportunity, he got the map and escaped to the ditch behind the house. The feeling of freedom was incredible. He could do anything he wanted now.

Striding down to the road toward the distant mountain, Sheep 93 vowed, "Someday, I'll return with a worthy answer for the sheep."

9 years and 3 months later, it was the day I met Sheep 93 and listened to his life story. At that time, I returned to the EIM with an invitation from Dragon 25, the king's ambassador now. He had helped many people speak again and made them change the name of the kingdom to EISA (Everyone Is Speaking Again.)

While we were walking in the royal garden, Sheep 93 emerged from the fence. He had sneaked in to talk to Dragon 25.

"Dear sir," Sheep 93 said with tears in his eyes. "I admire your story of changing the boring EIM kingdom to beautiful EISA. I want to change the sheep in my hometown. Please help!"

"Oh, my friend," Dragon 25 said. "Don't be so formal. Let's take a walk together, and we will talk like friends."

Then three of us strolled around the garden. Sheep 93 was emotional. He told us everything that happened since he escaped from the sheep palace.

After fleeing home, Sheep 93 traveled around the world in search of his life purpose. He used to be an assistant to the most talented businessmen, but the answer that we were born to make a lot of money did not satisfy him. The money he earned enabled him to try many things and enjoy a luxurious life around the world. However, the answer that we were born to enjoy everything in life was not enough for him. Next, he followed a monk into the woods and meditated but did not find a satisfactory answer.

Sheep 93 kept searching for his life purpose with his only companion: loneliness. When not finding the answer, he decided to return home to endure his fate of being sheared as an ordinary sheep. On the way home, he heard about Dragon 25, who breathed ink and changed an entire kingdom. That story moved Sheep 93's heart, and he tried everything to sneak into the palace and met us.

At that point, tears welled up in Sheep 93's eyes. Seeing that, Dragon 25 said nothing and hugged him tightly. I didn't know how it felt to be embraced by a dragon, but I guessed it was great because Sheep 93 cried louder as if he met his savior. Perhaps hugging Sheep 93 brought an incredible sensation, so Dragon 25 kept doing that for almost two hours. I bet that if the princess had not asked Dragon 25 to work, he would continue hugging until midnight.

"Hey, Sheep 93," the princess asked when Dragon 25 had gone. "Can I hug you?"

Sheep 93's face turned red. "Oh... If you don't mind, your highness. It's just that people never hug me like that."

So the princess embraced Sheep 93. Her face looked more satisfied than ever. 30 minutes later, the princess couldn't let go. Sheep 93's face now looked like a tomato, and he didn't dare to move. Not until the king came and asked the princess to have dinner did she let go.

"Hey, Sheep 93," the king asked when the princess had gone. "Can you give me a hug?"

What's going on here? Why did everyone love to hug Sheep 93 so much? As I thought, not until the queen asked the king to have dinner did he let go.

And how the story went next, you probably figured out. The queen, the maids, and the guards, everyone in the castle, hugged Sheep 93. They were all pleased!

"Hey, Sheep 93," I asked.

"What is it, Parrot 69? Do you want a hug too?"

"Oh no. Listening to your life story, then watching you hugging people made me remember Rabbit 28. In the past, she used to make people happy with her inventions, then one day she stopped inventing and looked for a way to create time."

"Really?" Sheep 93's eyes sparkled. "What happened next?"

I told Sheep 93 the story of Rabbit 28 meeting God and receiving her answer. When I finished, Sheep 93 did not ask anything, just hugged me.

I was timid, but I ignored it because now I knew why people loved to hug him so much. His wool was so soft, and I believed Sheep 93 was the most incredible hug pillow in the world. I bet if people found out this secret, they would pluck him naked without mercy.

"Thank you, Bird 69," said Sheep 93. "The Dragon 25's embrace has triggered something in me and wiped away my loneliness for years. The story of Rabbit 28 has enlightened me. Now I know the purpose of a sheep's life. Please send my thanks to Dragon 25 and Rabbit 28. I must return to my homeland now and save my people before it's too late."

We then said goodbye.

Exactly 9 months and 3 days later, I received a postcard from Sheep 93. He had opened a hugging coffee shop in his hometown. When customers came and hugged Sheep 93, you would get a discount. Unexpectedly, some people were willing to pay hundreds of Susu to be embraced by Sheep 93 all day. They said, "The meal is better with a friend. Coffee is better with a hug."

Sheep 93 did not take money for his hug, only for the coffee. Thanks to that idea, he recruited more sheep to help him. Their main job was to take care of their wool and give everyone the warmest hugs. Most of his customers had felt lonely in life for years. When they came and had someone to hug and to talk to, they were delighted.

Later, Sheep 93 launched a campaign that had never happened in Numagician: Free Hug. He often walked a herd of sheep on the street, giving everyone free warm hugs, then sold coffee. Thanks to that, his chain of hugging coffee shops became more and more popular in Numagician. He created an excellent life purpose for the sheep: Born to hug.

Of course, some people objected to Sheep 93's business because his "Born to hug" message severely impacted the old belief "born to be sheared". The sales of companies selling products from sheep wool dropped dramatically because many sheep wanted to work for Sheep 93 to give their hugs instead of being painfully sheared.

Due to the decreasing number of sheep volunteering to be sheared, humans were frightened. They entrusted Sheep 93's father with a noble mission to close the hugging coffee shops and re-teach his son. If he failed, he would be demoted and sheared as an ordinary sheep. Can you guess what happened next?

There was always a muscular sheep standing in front of any coffee shop of Sheep 93, and you could only enter the door after hugging him. To see his son, the father had to reluctantly do one thing for the first time in his life: Hug a stranger.

Sheep 93 was very attentive. He trained every sheep in his staff how to give a perfect hug. Therefore, when the muscular sheep hugged the father, his face became relaxed with pleasure. After that, the father was enveloped in his son's embrace. The father and son hugged each other for the whole night.

Next, Sheep 93's father decided to resign and help his son develop the remarkable chain of hugging coffee.

My lesson from Sheep 93 is: What comes from the heart will reach the heart. The fastest way for two souls to touch is a free hug!

82

Crocodile 82
Believe In Yourself

Would you like to be more confident?

Most numbers in Numagician are very confident. Perhaps in school, we have "Confidology," a compulsory subject for the graduation exam. Of course, some exceptions are lack of confidence, including me.

However, this story is about Crocodile 82, who failed this confident exam no less than 82 times. Still, later she became a professor of Confidology. Her research has helped thousands of people become exceedingly confident.

If I used to be very shy about my colorful fur, Crocodile 82 was shy about everything. She wanted to change everything, including her rough scales, short legs, and even her oversized jaw. Crocodile 82 had been through 82 cosmetic surgeries, and she was still not satisfied with her appearance. People would call her an *ugly fish* instead of a *crocodile*.

The first time I saw Crocodile 82 was in the class *You Are Gorgeous* of Antelope 97, and she did not stand out so much. It was not until Antelope 97 invited me to the

Anyone Can Praise contest as a reporter, and Crocodile 82 made a deep impression on me. She won the first prize with a record of 82 creative compliments that made people laugh happily.

When meeting a buffalo with tiny crooked horns, she praised, "Your horns make me think about two branches of a vibrant seed, which could pierce the hardest soil to reach the sun."

When meeting a fat cat with a huge belly, she praised, "Your belly is amazing. It makes me think completely differently about fat people. I can lay my head on it and relax all day."

When meeting an old female dog with no teeth, she praised, "Thanks to being toothless, your smile makes you look like a baby, and several decades younger. I wish to see that smile all year long."

Life is about giving and taking. Crocodile 82's excellent compliments in the contest helped everybody feel more confident, including herself. They not only cleared her self-doubt but also enabled the seeds of confidence to sprout.

Thanks to the course and contest of Antelope 97, Crocodile 82 had been changed. People no longer called her an ugly fish, and she even dreamed of organizing a similar course to help people like her. There was only one thing that bothered her. Therefore, she looked for Antelope 97 after the contest.

"Dear teacher," Crocodile 82 asked. "If we use compliments only, can everybody become confident, or are there exceptions?"

Antelope 97 nodded. "You are smart. Although most students feel more confident after taking one course, some people attended course after course with no better result."

"Do you know why?"

"Oh, the essence of self-confidence is to believe in yourself. Maybe my method is not good enough to make the students believe they are better than they think. It's a chance for you to develop your course."

"Thank you, teacher. I understand now." Crocodile 82 said and left.

Having a fondness for nature swimming, Crocodile 82 returned to her hometown, rented a large lake, and opened a *Confidology In Use* course. According to her philosophy, real confidence came when you went through challenges in reality, not in an exam of the school's confidology subject.

It was such a curious name that many people signed up for Crocodile 82's course, including many old students from the *You Are Gorgeous* classes. Thanks to my writing talent, I got a free ticket to join the first course of Crocodile 82.

On the first day of the *Confidology In Use* course, Crocodile 82 gave each student a big bag of fish food and required them to wear long pants. The mission was simple: Feeding the baby crocodiles without letting them tear your pants apart. Thanks to my colorful fur and my short legs, they allowed me to not wear pants.

If you were there with me, you would see a big lake divided into dozens of small pools. Each was 8 times longer than a male crocodile's tail and 2 times wider than a female crocodile's tail (that's how crocodiles measure things.) In each pool, there were 82 baby crocodiles, and each had 82 polished, sharp teeth. They were very greedy. As long as you had food, they would chase you from pool to pool until they tore your pants apart.

On the graduation day of the course, my whole body was in pain. The baby crocodile had bitten 82 of my feathers. However, I was delighted with the result.

Before going to the course, my colorful fur made me very shy. I didn't recognize that I had another secret fear which was swimming. Every time I jumped into the water, I shivered and felt like I was about to drown. Thanks to my colorful fur again, those baby crocodiles kept chasing me. I couldn't think of anything to do, so I just flapped my wings to escape.

Every day was the same. I was chased by the baby crocodiles tirelessly until I could swim even faster than them (that's why I survived.) Other students admired my swimming skills and asked me for help. That made me feel happier and more confident. The colorful fur was no longer a problem. It even brought me more friends (most of them were baby crocodiles.) The more I think about it, the more I see that Crocodile 92 is right.

Fear is contagious. When people are afraid of something, the fear will grow and cause them to lose self-confidence, leading to other fears. In contrast, when you can overcome a particular fear, the rest will gradually disappear.

That's why Crocodile 92 always creates experiences, forcing people to overcome at least one of their fears, and they will become more and more confident naturally.

Seed 85
Great Or Extinct?

As I flew over the Sahara desert in your world, I almost died. The heat there was 8.5 times hotter than the Sahava desert in Numagician. The thing that helped me survive was Seed 85. Don't get me wrong. It's not a miracle food or magical tool. It's a seed and also a number in Numagician.

Seed 85 had a plump body and a single pair of green hair, which made him look like a sapling. His life story inspired me to train my wings and be able to overcome that wild desert.

Each person in Seed 85's family had a unique specialty, including foreseeing the future and recalling their past lives. Many people don't believe in reincarnation, or the previous life, or the next life in your world. It is the same in Numagician, but Seed 85 insisted that those things were real. He told me his most impressive previous life was when he was born in an oak family in the Sahava desert of Numagician a million years ago.

Back then, Sahava was still the refuge of green forests. The trees were so overgrown that if you jumped from a plane with a broken parachute, you could survive. Also, you had to be a genius to sneak to the ground to listen to a conversation of several saplings.

"That's amazing," one sapling said. "Our mother nature is so kind to us."

"That's right," another sapling said. "Cool groundwater is flowing through our roots. How wonderful!"

"Exactly!" a fat sapling said with a satisfied voice. "Just drink and enjoy!"

Many other plants also nodded their leaves. They believed that the delicious and nutritious groundwater would naturally flow through their roots forever. Meanwhile, one of the smallest trees fell silent. That was Seed 85. From a seed, he grew up to be a small oak tree. You might assume that his confidence was equal to his tiny body.

"I don't think so," said Seed 85. "My grandpa said nothing would last forever. One day the water will run out. If you enjoy drinking now and forget to develop a healthy root, you will go extinct."

"Extinct?" the fat sapling laughed. "You said like an old man. Only dinosaurs went extinct. This pure water has nourished our forest for thousands of years. It can't disappear!"

"That's right!" The whole group of saplings agreed with him.

Seed 85 said nothing. He just muttered and ignored them.

Since that day, his friends had focused on developing a huge trunk, big branches, and large leaves to get more sunshine and show off their bodies. Seed 85 did the opposite. He used most of the nutrition he got from the water to develop the roots. Therefore, he could reach deeper into the ground. Every time he went to a new depth and discovered a new groundwater branch, a small feeling of victory made him happy.

Although many times Seed 85 encountered rocks or hard areas with no water, he was not discouraged. His grandpa once said if you kept going with persistence, you would always win in the end. Seed 85 dreamed of exploring the deepest underground area that no one had been before.

Time passed by. Mother nature continued to favor the forest. The little Seed 85 now became a mature oak tree. He got married, raised baby trees, and kept his dream. Following his philosophy, the whole oak family focused on developing healthy roots to sneak into deeper grounds. They had incredible experiences that other plants would not know if they just concentrated on the ground's surface.

At last, the judgment day had come. A terrible earthquake destroyed many sources of groundwater. The forest which had been protected by mother nature for a thousand years now had to face the greatest challenge of life. The water ran out and many trees fell down. There were young trees that chatted together in the past, but now only a few remained under the scorching sun.

"Oh no!" said the fat tree. "The ground has cracked, we're going to die!"

Then he collapsed, his weak root wasn't able to hold his huge trunk.

Not far from that fat tree, Seed 85 encouraged his family to stand firm. This was the moment they had to be more persistent than ever, to not only overcome the earthquake, but also conquer new depths to find water.

Till this day, the oak growing in the Sahava desert of Numagician had become legend.

When Seed 85 told me that past life story, I was enlightened. Thanks to the electronic spider network, my bird forest was very advanced at that time. You could do everything at home by just pressing a button, including buying food, drinks, books, and clothes. They would deliver to your door in no time.

People rarely left their house for a walk. They traveled by Grabbird, a transportation service like Grabbike here. Those convenient things gradually made us as fat as penguins, and no one could fly anymore. If something terrible happens to the forest now, how can we escape?

Believing in the warning of Seed 85, I bought a flying practice machine and began to train my wings early in the morning. Many people called me crazy because they thought flying was no longer needed in this era. However, I kept training and believed that someday something bad would happen to the forest. My ability to fly with my own wings would be helpful.

Finally, that day had come, but that 'something bad' did not happen to the forest. It happened to me. My storytelling talent reached the king's ears. He asked me to come to the palace and motivate princess Nana to love drawing again. I wrote all the details of that terrible incident in the book *Numagician - Awaken Your Super Creative Artist Within*. See you there.

Later, I got lost in your world and fell right back into the Sahara desert. Fortunately, my trained wings helped me fly over the desert. I would have become a grilled bird if I used my feet to walk there.

I was lost again in the desert. At the most exhausting moment, I saw an oak tree. It immediately reminded me of Seed 85's story and inspired me to flap my wings with a belief: Keep going, and victory will be yours; green grass fields are awaiting for you at the edge of the desert.

And I did it. The proof is that I'm still here to write this diary. Later, Google helped me find the information about that oak tree. It is called the Ténéré, known as the largest oak tree in the Sahara desert. Some magazines praised it as the *only nature object* marked on the Sahara map.

That oak tree amazed the scientist because it could stand alone in the desert, without any tree companions for a radius of 400 km. They dug a nearby well and surprisingly discovered its root plunged 36 meters into the ground to find water. That depth is equivalent to the height of a 10-story building. It is admirable, isn't it?

The Oil Barrel Secret In Story Writing

Well, reading here, you may wonder, "Is that all? Where are the stories of other numbers?"

The answer is, I'm still writing about them. But why don't you write about them yourself? It is not as difficult as you think.

When I was a kid, I got a bad score of 4/10 in Literature. Therefore, I believed that writing stories was too difficult. If someone asked me to tell a story, I didn't know where to start. When I found the oil barrel secret, everything changed. What is the oil barrel secret?

Once upon a time, there was an army that had to march through the Sahara desert. To ensure the safety of his soldiers, the general came up with an idea. He recruited a squad of the most elite soldiers and provided them wagons filled with many empty oil barrels. Their mission was to find a safe way to drop oil barrels as markers every 5 kilometers. Thanks to that, the entire army could march through the desert easily. Instead of walking tiredly, facing a vast desert ahead, the soldiers were always eager to look for their target: the next empty oil barrel.

Writing stories is very similar. If you don't know where to start, it's not because you are bad at storytelling. It's because you have not found your empty oil barrels, which are specific questions to help you create a story.

Before I tell you how I discovered the golden questions that helped me create many interesting stories, let's read an ordinary story that I wrote in the past.

The original one

There was a big fat dog. While living happily, his owner kicked him out of the house. He was very sad, just sitting there and gnawing on a bone all his life.

End of story!

It's such a weird story without a beginning or an end. Can you believe that it took me half an hour to create it? Now, take a look at the improved version of the story after using the golden questions.

The improved version

In 2089, in New York City, people invented a dog muzzle called Gau Gau, which helps any dog speak like a human and communicate effectively with each other.

There was a big fat dog, living happily with his boss. One day, the boss brought home a Gau Gau muzzle, but the dog refused to wear it and ran away.

While running away, he fell into a sewer and found a gang of dogs. They were preparing to start a revolution called The Rise Of The Dogs.

What happened next? See you in the sequel. If you are curious about the fate of that dog, then the golden questions work! So what are those questions anyway?

The golden questions in story writing

Context: Where did the story happen? In which era? Was there anything similar or more interesting than what happened in your era?

Character: Who was your main character? Did he have anything similar or different to anyone? What was his goal?

Conflict: What happened unexpectedly? What prevented the main character from achieving his goal? How did he react?

Catastrophe: What catastrophe did the character's action lead to? After that, how did he react? What was next?

Closing: How did the story end? Was it a happy ending or something unclear? What was the lesson for the readers?

From now on, if you want to create a story, choose any character, a cat, a monkey, a pig, or whatever, then answer those questions one by one. They will help you create an interesting storyline.

Do you need more examples? Let's look at the one below to understand more about these golden questions.

The first version

A student found out that he was a wizard. He traveled and helped people—end of the story.

The improved version

Context: Great Britain, modern times.

Character: An orphan boy who was living with his aunt and uncle. No one liked him. His goal was to live a normal life.

Conflict: On his 11th birthday, he received a mysterious letter, but his family prevented him from reading it. He tried so hard that they moved to a house in the middle of the ocean.

Catastrophe: At midnight, a big muscular man broke the door and told him that it was the magical school's admission letter. He was a wizard. Later, he followed that man, not knowing that they started a dangerous journey to deal with the dark forces that murdered his parents in the past.

Closing: What happened next? Please read the Harry Potter series.

As you can see, these golden questions were not invented by me. I learned them from master story writers all over the world. They also used them.

Of course, there are many versions of questions. Those basic questions above will help you write a good storyline. There are a few more steps to develop it into a detailed story with more characters and twists, and you can even make a screenplay!

Every journey starts with a single step. And this is your first step to awaken the inspiring storyteller within you. Let's practice creating stories with the other numbers at the end of this book.

Just do, then it will be done.

Just go, then you will be there.

Looking forward to your good news.

Fususu

Practice Story Writing

Now you can use the golden questions below to create compelling stories for the other numbers in Numagician.

Context: Where did the story happen? In which era? Was there anything similar or more interesting than what happened in your era?

Character: Who was your main character? Did he have anything that was similar or different to anyone? What was his goal?

Conflict: What happened unexpectedly? What prevented the main character from achieving his goal? How did he react?

Catastrophe: What catastrophe did the character's action lead to? After that, how did he react? What was next?

Closing: How did the story end? Was it a happy ending or something unclear? What was the lesson for the readers?

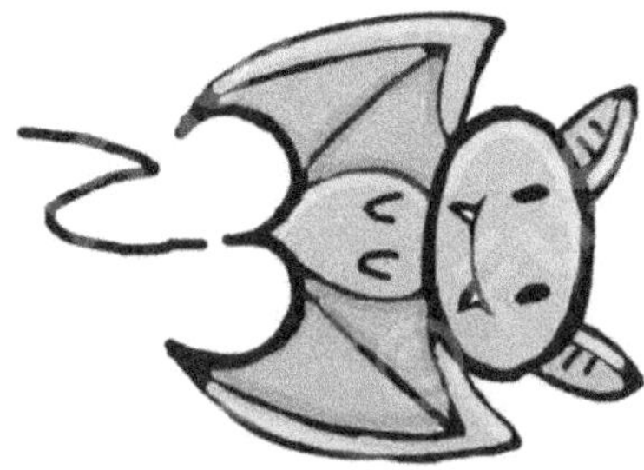

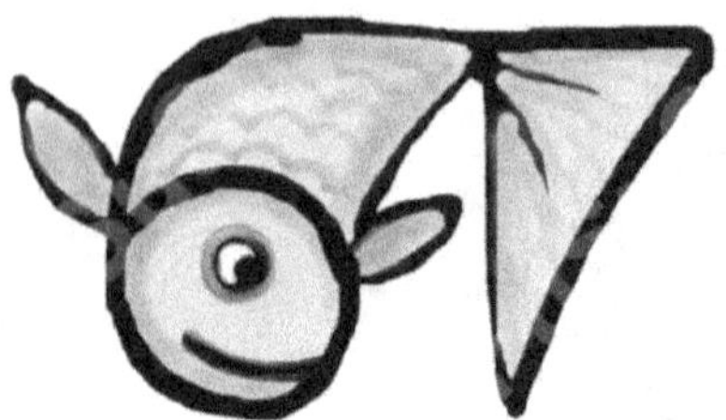

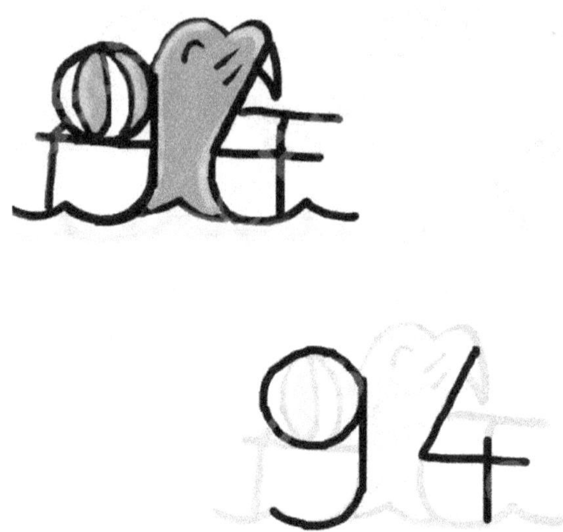

About the Author

Fususu is the pen name of Nguyen Chu Nam Phuong. He graduated from elementary school with a bad score of 4/10 in Literature. Still, he has become an author with 7 published books, and three of them have become bestsellers in Vietnam for years. Although his English was not so good, he translated all of his books into English.

Despite being an introvert and afraid of speaking, he became a public speaker with thousands of hours of speaking. He is the founder of ACI Toastmasters Online, also the first Worldclass Speaking Coach in Vietnam, certified by Craig Valentine, the 1999 World Champion of Public Speaking.

From his humble start to great successes in many areas, Fususu believes that everything is possible. God had given you a genius brain, but he just forgot to send the manual. All you need is the key to unlock your potential, and the 10-year long way of Fususu could become your shortcut in his books.

www.ingramcontent.com/pod-product-compliance
Lightning Source LLC
Chambersburg PA
CBHW050527160726
48003CB00001B/487